# The Suite Life
## of Zack & Cody

# Star Crazy

Adapted by Laurie McElroy

Based on the series created by Danny Kallis & Jim Geoghan

Based on the episode, "Rock Star in the House," Written by Jeny Quine & Howard Nemetz

DISNEY
CHANNEL

DISNEY
PRESS

New York

Printed in the United States of America

First Edition
1 3 5 7 9 10 8 6 4 2

Library of Congress Catalog Card Number on file.

ISBN-13: 978-14231-0465-0
ISBN-10: 1-4231-0465-X
For more Disney Press fun, visit www.disneybooks.com
Visit DisneyChannel.com

# Chapter 1

Zack and Cody Martin stepped off the elevator with their mother, Carey, to find the normally calm and dignified lobby of the Tipton Hotel filled with the sounds of high-pitched screams and squeals. Dozens of teen girls had surrounded the building, waving handmade signs and screaming.

Zack and Cody eyed each other nervously. When there was trouble at the Tipton, the twins were almost always the cause. Had they done something to create this chaos without knowing it?

They tried to obey the rules. Really, they did. After all, their mother was a professional singer who performed regularly in the hotel ballroom. That meant that they got to live in a beautiful suite on the twenty-third floor of one of Boston's fanciest hotels. That was one of the perks included in her contract.

And it was a *great* perk! Zack and Cody loved living in the Tipton, but the hotel manager, Mr. Moseby, didn't always love them. In fact, he sometimes called them, "double trouble."

But now his attention was on two girls he had found hiding behind a plant in the lobby. He handed them over to a bellboy. "Please remove these two and check behind the couches for more," he said with a disgusted sniff.

Just then a duffle bag in the luggage-check area let out a sneeze.

Carey raised her eyebrows. "I think that bag has a cold," she said.

The black-and-red bag started to move, inching away from them, but Mr. Moseby was too fast. He grabbed the handle and unzipped the bag. There was a girl hiding inside.

"Out!" he demanded. "And take your matching duffel friend with you," he said, pointing to an identical bag.

The two duffel bags hopped dejectedly toward the door together.

"What are all of these girls here for?" Cody asked.

"We happen to have a very famous guest checking in this afternoon," Mr. Moseby sighed. He had tried to keep the news from everyone—especially the twins—but word clearly had gotten out. The hotel had been besieged by squealing girls since dawn, and Mr. Moseby had developed a raging headache.

Carey watched two more girls do their best to sneak past a security guard, and she shook her head in amazement. "It's so silly how insane women get when it comes to musicians."

"Who is it?" Zack asked Mr. Moseby, wondering who could manage to get so many girls so excited.

"That McCartney fellow," Mr. Moseby said.

Carey gasped. "Paul McCartney?" Suddenly getting insane over a musician didn't seem silly at all.

She started jumping up and down,

clapping her hands and screaming. "I love Paul McCartney!"

"Who's he?" Cody asked. He had never seen his mother go crazy for a rock star before. It was a little disturbing to see her act like a lovesick teenager.

"Not *Paul* McCartney," Mr. Moseby explained. "*Jesse* McCartney."

Now it was Carey's turn to be confused. "Who's he?" she asked.

But Zack and Cody suddenly understood. "Jesse Mac" was a household name in the teen world with a long list of top-ten songs, and an even longer list of fans.

❖ ❖ ❖

Across the lobby, Maddie Fitzpatrick had just arrived for her after-school job at the hotel's candy counter. London Tipton (as in

Tipton Hotel) leaned on the counter looking dreamily at a picture of Jesse McCartney on the glossy cover of a teen magazine and sighing over how completely gorgeous he was.

"I can't believe all these girls are screaming for Jesse McCartney," Maddie said with a frown. "It's so lame."

"And delusional," London agreed, haughtily flipping her long black hair over her shoulder. "They all think they have a shot with Jesse, when clearly he and I are meant to be."

She held the magazine up next to her face so that Maddie could see for herself what a great couple they would be. Then London lowered the magazine and gazed at his picture again with a loving sigh.

The only very slight problem was that a lot of other girls also thought that they would make a perfect couple with Jesse McCartney. London didn't mind a little competition, especially when she knew she could outshine them all, but she didn't want Jesse to be distracted by all those other hopefuls.

London knew Maddie wasn't a threat, especially when Maddie was wearing her school uniform—a blue shirt, boring plaid skirt, and an even more boring plaid tie. But some of these screaming girls were wearing semicute outfits, and London really wanted them to go away.

London herself always wore the latest fashions, and today she had dressed up even more than usual. She wore a black sequined top and a faux-fur shrug—an incredibly fashion-forward outfit that was specifically designed to get Jesse's attention.

And if that didn't work—well, she had

an enormous closet full of adorable clothes. She drifted off into a pleasant daydream in which she modeled a series of outfits for Jesse and he marveled at how beautiful and fashionable she was. . . .

These delightful thoughts were interrupted by a hand tapping her on the shoulder.

"Do you know where the manager's office is?" a male voice asked.

London didn't even bother to look at the person standing behind her. She pointed dismissively. "Over there," she snapped. Who did this person think he was, bothering her when she was dreaming about her future with Jesse?

Maddie's jaw dropped as she watched the guy walk away. London had just totally dissed her idol.

"Wasn't that Jesse McCartney?" Maddie asked.

London's eyes got wide, and all of a sudden she realized whose voice that was. She let out a little shocked gasp just before she hit the floor with a thud. London had fainted!

# Chapter 2

Arwin, the hotel handyman, was tinkering with a machine in his basement office. "Three, two, one . . . incoming!" he shouted, popping a piece of bread into a toaster and flipping a switch. "Aha!"

Cody walked in carrying a cardboard box. Everyone else at the Tipton might be obsessing about a rock star, but he was worrying about something that was far more important—his science project.

"Hey, Cody!" Arwin said excitedly. "You're just in time to test out my new invention. I call it the Catapult Toaster. See, now you can sit at the table and relax and let the toast come . . ."

Arwin pushed a button on a remote control and the catapult arm flipped up, tossing his toast right into his face.

". . . to you," he finished with a sigh. He had been tinkering with this project for a while, but he hadn't quite worked out all the kinks yet.

Cody brushed bread crumbs off Arwin's shoulder, but he had other things on his mind besides toast. If he wanted to win his science contest, he didn't have time to worry about someone else's invention.

"Listen, Arwin, I was wondering if I could use some of your tools," Cody said.

"I'm entered in Boston's Junior Science Contest, and my project still needs a lot of work."

"Sure, sure," Arwin said, rubbing his hands together with delight. He absolutely loved science projects. "What are you making?"

Cody took his project out of the box and spread the parts out on Arwin's worktable. They didn't look like much yet, but when they were assembled Cody was sure he'd have a good chance of winning. "It's gonna be a laser," he explained.

"Ah, cool!" Arwin said, examining the project. "You know, I entered a science contest at my school once."

"Yeah? Did you win?" Cody asked.

"Well, I would have. But one lousy explosion and they ban you for life," Arwin said, still smarting from the unfairness of it all. In his own defense, he added, "That gym needed a pool anyway."

Then he noticed the horrified expression that had appeared on Cody's face. "I'm sure you'll do better with your project," he said quickly.

"I better," Cody answered. He had already decided that getting into the right college, finding the right career, and establishing a successful future depended on winning this contest.

"I've just got to win this science award," he went on, a determined look in his eye. "Then I can get into MIT, invent a nanobot that eats oil spills, and be able to retire comfortably while taking care of my aging mother and paying my brother's bail money."

Arwin's forehead wrinkled in confusion. "Zack's in jail?" he asked.

"Not yet," Cody said with a frown.

"Oh," Arwin said, nodding.

You could call Zack the fun-loving twin, and he didn't mind if he got into trouble having it; in fact, getting into a little trouble made things even more fun.

Cody, on the other hand, was more serious. He studied harder, entered academic contests, and often found himself trying to keep his brother out of trouble. He figured that watching out for Zack was something he'd be doing long into adulthood. So a lot was riding on this science project. It had to be absolutely perfect.

Cody grabbed a screwdriver and started to tinker.

Arwin peered over Cody's shoulder. His fingers itched to grab the screwdriver and take over.

"Well, if you need any help I'm right

here," he said. "After all, I am a professional inventor."

Then he leaned back in his chair with a satisfied smile and put his hands behind his head.

Just then, a couple of pats of butter shot out of the catapult and hit Arwin in the face. He blinked and did his best to make a graceful recovery. He cleared his throat, picked up the toast from the floor, and wiped the butter off his face with it before offering it to Cody.

"Buttered toast?" he asked.

Cody eyed the toast with disgust and took a giant step back.

❖❖❖

After school the next day, Maddie and London walked through the hotel lobby discussing the best way to meet Jesse McCartney. London had already managed to get one of the hotel employees to slip her Jesse's daily schedule. They knew he would be rehearsing in the ballroom that afternoon. And now that they knew where he would be, it seemed like a simple matter to track him down and casually start talking to him. After all, who knew where a little friendly conversation could lead?

That, of course, was only the first part of the plan. As for the next part . . . well, the two girls had very different ideas about what should happen next.

London was sure that Jesse would fall in love with her the minute they started talking. Maddie had another goal: she wanted to get a scoop about Jesse for her school newspaper. The singer had so many fans at her school—she would really make her mark as a journalist if she could get an exclusive photo, or maybe even a one-on-one interview!

"Okay, I really need a picture of Jesse McCartney for my school newspaper," Maddie reminded London. She had a camera around her neck.

"Don't worry," London assured her confidently. "I'll get us in to see him rehearse. After all, he's a celebrity, I'm a celebrity. We're first celebrities, once removed."

Maddie tried not to roll her eyes. The only thing that made London a celebrity was her money.

London smoothed her long, dark hair, drawing attention to the tiara she wore. She had chosen this sparkly accessory very carefully. She knew Jesse would take one look at her and think she looked like a princess. The glittering tiara matched her pink, beaded choker and the shiny pink sequins on her top.

Mr. Moseby cut them off just before they got to the ballroom. "You go in there, and you'll be removed," he said firmly.

London stamped her foot. This was her hotel, not Mr. Moseby's. And she was used to getting her way—in everything.

"My father won't stand for this," she said, pouting.

Mr. Moseby ignored this and firmly led the girls away from the ballroom. "Actually, I just received a fax from your father asking that you be kept away from all celebrities staying at the hotel."

He gave London a meaningful look. "He doesn't want a repeat of the Orlando Bloom incident."

London tossed her head impatiently. So she had gone a little overboard, but Orlando didn't suffer any *permanent* damage. After a few months, he even said he could see the humor of it all.

"Just tell Daddy it's different this time," she said.

Mr. Moseby flipped through a stack of papers, muttering to himself as he read. "Different this time . . . ah, here we are," he said, finding the right page and reading again. "'It's not different. You are clearly obsessed with 'insert celebrity name here,' and if you continue to harass 'insert celebrity name here,' you will be sent to 'insert boarding school name here.'"

London fumed. "That's it. If he doesn't let me see Jesse, I'll—"

Mr. Moseby cut her off, flipping through his faxes again. "I've got 'run away,' 'scream at the top of my lungs,' or 'hold my breath until I turn blue.'"

Clearly, London's father had heard these threats before and was ready with a few threats of his own.

Mr. Moseby looked up from his papers with a big smile. "Which will it be?" he asked.

"Do you always have to do everything that Daddy tells you to?" London whined.

"Of course I do," he answered. "Until such time that your father tells me I don't." He turned on his heel and left.

London watched him walk away and then turned to Maddie. "I have to get in there to meet my future husband," she insisted, already starting to form a plan.

Maddie hesitated. She was always telling herself to stay out of London's crazy schemes, but she always ended up right in the middle of them, anyway. And she really, really wanted that photograph for the school paper.

"Okay, but we're not doing anything stupid, right?" she asked.

"No," London answered with a gleam in her eye.

"Okay," Maddie agreed. But was that determination in London's eyes or was it obsession, she wondered. *What have I gotten myself into?*

# Chapter 3

Maddie had her answer an hour later. After Mr. Moseby stopped them from checking out Jesse's rehearsal, London came up with a plan. London wasn't about to let Mr. Moseby or her father's silly faxes keep her from the rock star of her dreams. How could Jesse marry her if they never even had a chance to meet?

The two girls, dressed as Tipton waiters—

complete with tuxedo pants, bow ties, jackets, and white gloves—wheeled a food cart into the ballroom. They each wore a fake mustache and had tucked their hair into caps. No one would guess that these two guys were female Jesse McCartney fans in disguise—or so they hoped.

Jesse was onstage, ready to begin his rehearsal.

"I feel so stupid," Maddie said to London.

Jesse stepped up to the microphone. "Check. Check. One. Two, two."

London grabbed Maddie's arm and started jumping up and down. "It's him!" she squealed. "It's him!"

A stagehand passing by with a guitar shot them a look. They weren't exactly acting like waiters.

Maddie deepened her voice to sound like a guy. "He's really excited about the soup of the day," she explained to the stagehand, and then hissed at London through clenched teeth. "Will you calm down? He's just a regular guy like you and me. . . ."

Jesse started to sing the opening notes to a song.

Maddie turned toward him, totally mesmerized. "With the voice of an angel," she said in a whisper, walking toward the stage. Her knees were suddenly weak.

London pulled her back. She recognized that lovesick look—she saw it in the mirror whenever she thought about Jesse. "Hey, don't get any funny ideas. Jesse is mine," she warned Maddie.

Jesse had just noticed the two "waiters" and signaled in London's direction.

"Look, he's gesturing to me!" she said breathlessly, putting her hand over her heart. "I think he wants to propose."

Maddie shook her head. "He's pointing at the water, dingbat," she said sarcastically. "He thinks you're a waiter."

"Why would he think that?" London asked. She looked down at herself. "Oh, right," she said, remembering.

London walked toward Jesse holding the water glass in both hands. This was it! Her chance to meet her idol in person, to dazzle him with her wit and beauty, and to start them down the road to true love . . .

She was shaking so much that most of the water ended up on the floor. By the time she handed the glass to Jesse, it was almost empty.

"Thanks, man," Jesse said, giving the waiter an odd look. After all, most waiters didn't hyperventilate when they handed him a drink! He shrugged and drank the tiny bit of water left in the glass.

London ran back to Maddie and squealed. "He called me man!" She pointed from herself to Jesse and back again. "We are *so* meant to be!"

Maddie and London tried to remember that they were supposed to be waiters, but they totally lost it when Jesse started to rehearse his latest hit—a beautiful love song. They swayed and danced and imagined that Jesse was singing directly to them. The only problem was that Jesse and his guitarist were shooting weird looks in their direction. Maddie and London weren't acting like waiters, they were acting like fans—girl fans.

When Jesse came to the end of his song, the girls broke into screams and applause. Then Maddie remembered who she was supposed to be.

"Great set, man," she said in the deepest voice she could muster.

"Try the soup," London growled, puffing her chest out like a guy.

Mr. Moseby came into the ballroom to check on things. "Is everything all right in here? No screaming girls?"

"No, but there, there were a couple of screaming waiters," Jesse said, pointing.

Mr. Moseby turned, but he didn't see any waiters—just a food cart. He turned back to the stage just in time for Maddie and London to wheel themselves out of the ballroom. They were hiding under the cart's tablecloth!

❖❖❖

Arwin stood over Cody, watching him work on his project.

". . . So if I just connect the blue wire to the red wire," Cody said to himself.

Arwin squeaked, then put a hand over his mouth. He had promised to let Cody work on his project all on his own. But it was hard not to say anything.

"What's the matter?" Cody asked.

"Nothing. Nothing. Nothing," Arwin babbled nervously. "No, you do it your way. Your way. Connect whatever wires you want. The red to the blue or the yellow to the blue. I'd do the yellow to the blue, but that's just me. You need to follow your heart."

Cody nodded. He really appreciated the way Arwin was holding himself back, letting Cody figure out this project on his own, not telling him what to do . . .

But Arwin couldn't help saying one more thing: "Yellow to blue."

Cody sighed. "Arwin, I told you I'm supposed to do this project myself. If I get help from someone else, it's cheating."

"I know, I know, I know," Arwin said. "I promise not to say anything else. My lips are sealed." Then he had a thought. "Do you want me to actually seal them? Because I can." Arwin picked up a giant glue gun and pointed it at his mouth.

"Hey, guys," Cody's mom said as she came into the office in search of Cody.

"Hey! Carey!" Arwin said, trying to lean on a chair nonchalantly. "How you doing?" But the chair was on wheels, and Arwin fell to the floor with a thud.

"Are you okay?" Carey asked, helping him up.

Arwin was completely flustered. He had a major crush on the twins' mom. "Wow. Uh," was all he managed to say in response.

Cody rolled his eyes. Arwin was just as bad as the screaming girls in the lobby. "Smooth," he said sarcastically.

"It's okay, Arwin," Carey said with a laugh. "I just came down to tell Cody it's time for lunch."

"Okay," Cody said. "Let me just test it out once." Cody connected the blue wire to the red wire and pushed a button on his laser.

There was a pop, then a flash of pink followed by lots of smoke. Cody jumped into his mother's arms. Arwin grabbed the fire extinguisher and soaked the laser with foam just as it exploded.

"Oh, no, it's ruined!" Cody cried, waving the smoke away and looking down at what remained of his science project. It was beyond fixing—he'd have to start all over. "I'll never win the science award now."

"Honey, it's okay. You still have time," Carey said. "Maybe you should try something a little simpler, like the volcano we talked about."

Cody slumped in his chair and shook his head. His mother didn't understand—his project had to be the best. And a volcano wasn't going to cut it.

"Like a stupid volcano is going to win," he muttered under his breath.

"Mine did get honorable mention in the Mini Madame Curie Competition," she answered.

"Those were simpler times," Cody said.

Arwin was stuck on the idea of Carey in a science competition. Now he liked her even more. "You were a science geek?" He lost control of the fire extinguisher, sending more foam into the air.

Carey ignored him. "My point is, it doesn't matter if you win. All that matters is that you do your best."

"Well, my best isn't going to win me a Nobel Prize, pay for your nursing home, or get Zack out of jail," Cody said, looking up at her.

Carey's voice rose in alarm. "Zack's in jail?"

Cody and Arwin answered at the same time. "Not yet."

# Chapter 4

A security guard blocked the entrance to Jesse's hotel room and drove a group of screaming teenage girls toward the elevator. A maid pushed her cart down the hall without noticing that she had picked up a passenger.

Hiding under the food cart had given Maddie an idea, so she had crawled onto the bottom shelf of the maid's cart and now was hidden by a sheet.

The maid stopped in front of Jesse's room and opened the door. When she headed into the bathroom with a stack of clean towels, Maddie saw her chance and grabbed it. She rolled off the cart and into the room.

After hearing Jesse sing in person, the idea of all those girls screaming for him wasn't quite so lame. Maddie's eyes lit up when she spotted Jesse's blue plaid bathrobe draped over the end of his bed. She picked it up and hugged it to her, taking a big sniff of Jesse's scent.

She didn't notice London push her way through the air vent near the ceiling and drop to the floor.

The girls backed into each other and turned with hushed screams. "What are you doing here?" they asked each other at the same time.

"Be quiet," Maddie said in a whisper. "The maid's in the bathroom."

London took in Maddie's outfit. Hmm, she thought, something's different here. . . .

Maddie wasn't wearing her school uniform. She was dressed up in a purple tie-dyed T-shirt and jeans with a cool, sheer wrap skirt over them!

It was hard to believe, but she actually looked . . . cute! London narrowed her eyes. She knew what *that* meant!

"You're trying to steal Jesse from me!" London hissed.

"Oh, please," Maddie answered, pretending to be cool to Jesse's charms. "I'm here for purely journalistic purposes."

"Then why are you hugging his bathrobe?" London demanded.

Maddie really had no excuse, but she made one up anyway. "I collect plaid," she said defiantly.

London was ready with a comeback, but just then the maid came back into the room, and the girls ducked behind the bed. As soon as the maid put the used towels on her cart and closed the door behind her, the girls popped back up.

"She's gone," Maddie said.

"Good! Now give me my husband's bathrobe!" London demanded.

Maddie hugged the robe tighter. London grabbed a sleeve and tugged. Maddie pulled back.

They were too busy fighting to notice Zack crawl through the same air vent that London had used. Just as he dropped to the floor, the girls ripped the bathrobe in two.

"Now look what you did!" Maddie yelled accusingly.

Zack stepped forward and took the two halves of the bathrobe. "I'll take that," he said. "I'm selling his stuff on the street. One girl gave me thirty bucks for the tissue he spit his gum into."

He threw the robe over his shoulder and headed toward the bathroom. "There's big money in obsession."

"You should be ashamed of yourself," London called after him.

"Yeah," Maddie agreed, walking over to Jesse's dresser. She opened a drawer and began rummaging through it.

"Sneaking into someone's room, invading their privacy, going through their personal belongings . . . Ooh," she squealed, picking up a pair of red boxer shorts. "He's a boxer guy!"

Zack came back into the bedroom with a stack of clean towels and a few other items he'd picked up in his search. "Darn! The maid got all the dirty towels. Now I have to start from scratch."

He crumpled the towels into a ball and liberally sprayed them with Jesse's cologne. Then he added a few hairs from Jesse's hairbrush.

"What are you doing?" Maddie asked, totally confused.

"There! Now it's been used by Jesse McCartney," Zack explained.

"I'll give you fifty bucks for it," London said quickly.

"London!" Maddie cried in disbelief. "You just saw Zack dirty it himself."

"Fine." London snapped. Then she paused to reconsider. "Thirty," she said to Zack.

Before Zack could start negotiating, they

heard Jesse's voice out in the hall. He was talking to his security guards. "Hey, guys, how's it going?" he asked.

Maddie and London started to jump up and down with excitement. In a few seconds they would actually get to meet him.

"Pretty good, Mr. McCartney," the security guard answered.

"It's him! It's him!" Maddie squealed. "How do I look?"

"Penniless, and your hair is messed up," London answered, reaching out and messing up Maddie's hair.

Maddie stared at her, ready to fight, but then she heard Mr. Moseby's voice.

"I told you, we have vigilant security," he said. "No one is getting into this room. Not even a mouse."

"Rats!" Zack whispered. "It's Moseby."

Getting to meet Jesse was one thing, but

no one wanted to have to face Mr. Moseby. He had told them all to stay away from Jesse, or else. They needed to get out of that room, and fast. But they looked at the door and then at each other as they realized— there was no way out!

# Chapter 5

Mr. Moseby escorted Jesse into his hotel room and looked around. Everything seemed to be neat and in order.

"I'm terribly sorry about all the unruly fans," he said, putting a gift basket down on the table. "I've ordered a SWAT team for this evening."

"No biggie," Jesse said with a shrug. "You gotta get used to it. You'd be surprised what some of these fans will do." He sat on the edge of his bed, kicked off his shoes, and dropped his bracelet into the drawer of his bedside table. He sighed. Even though he was grateful that he had so many fans, it felt good to be by himself for a while to relax. "I'm going to shower and take a nap before the show."

From his hiding place under the bed, Zack spotted Jesse's shoe and saw dollar signs— lots of them. He forgot about Mr. Moseby and reached out to drag the shoe under the bed, but Maddie grabbed his wrist and pulled it back.

Jesse headed into the bathroom. After a moment, he came back out, looking puzzled. "Excuse me, but there don't seem to be any towels."

"Oh, dear . . ." Mr. Moseby said with an embarrassed laugh. He hated it when Tipton guests didn't have everything they needed. After all, the Tipton was one of the best hotels in the country. "I'm terribly sorry once again. I'll get you the towels myself."

"Thanks, just leave them by the bathroom door," Jesse said, closing the door behind him.

"As you wish," Mr. Moseby said. As he left the room, Mr. Moseby banged right into the back of a huge security guard. Good, he thought. At least our star guest won't be bothered by any of his obnoxious fans while he's staying with us!

But as soon as the hotel manager was gone, Maddie, London, and Zack crawled out from under the bed.

London stared at the closed bathroom door. Just one thin section of wood separated her from the guy of her dreams! The thought seemed to send her into a trance. She started walking toward the bathroom as if she were under a spell. In the meantime, Zack was busy rummaging through Jesse's bedside table.

"Where are you going?" Maddie asked London.

"Don't you think it will make a cute story for the press when they find out Jesse and I first met while he was flossing?" London answered.

Maddie stared at her with an "are you crazy?" look. Following Jesse into the bathroom was definitely taking things too far. They were heading into Orlando Bloom territory.

"I think it will make a cute story for the police," Maddie answered. "Come on!"

She grabbed London's arm and pulled her toward the chair under the vent. They had to get out of there before Mr. Moseby came back with the towels and caught them.

Zack slammed the drawer shut and ran out with them. He had Jesse's bracelet in his hand.

❖❖❖

Cody sat behind Arwin's worktable. He was totally frustrated. Arwin stood behind him with his hand over his mouth.

Cody had been working on his new laser all day, and it still wasn't right. He connected two more wires, and absolutely nothing happened.

"Nothing!" he shouted, throwing his hands up into the air. "Stupid laser will never work." He kicked the leg of the table. "I wish I could fix it just so I could use it to destroy it."

Arwin's face lit up. He had been doing his very best to stay quiet and let Cody make his own mistakes all afternoon, but when it came to destroying things he just couldn't help saying something. He got excited.

"I like the way your mind works," he said with enthusiasm. "All you have to do is make some minor adjustments and you'll win hands down."

"Okay," Cody said slowly. He stared at his laser again, touching the different parts, trying to focus. "Let's see . . . The copper chloride is supposed to be heated here by connecting the power sources to the red wire."

"Blue," Arwin said, coughing into his hand.

Cody turned to him, then looked back at his project. "I mean, the blue wire?" he asked hesitantly.

Arwin gave him a silent thumbs-up.

Cody nodded. He was starting to under-

"What are all of these girls here for?" Cody asked
Mr. Moseby, referring to the crowd outside.

"I can't believe all these girls are screaming over
Jesse McCartney," Maddie said.

"I have to get in there to meet my future husband,"
London said, determined to get into Jesse's rehearsal.

"The voice of an angel," a disguised
Maddie said when she heard Jesse singing.

"I'm selling his stuff on the street," Zack explained as he took Jesse's plaid pajamas from the girls.

Zack, Maddie, and London are about to be caught—in Jesse's room!

"That's Jesse's lucky bracelet!" Maddie cried out,
seeing what Zack had stolen.

When the security guards are called,
Zack has to charm his way out of another mess!

stand—he thought. "So the discharge tube couples the laser medium with the optical cavity."

Arwin coughed into his hand again. "Not quite." He kept coughing, trying to cover the fact that he was helping. "You forgot the buffer gas."

"That means I have to weld it," Cody said.

Arwin touched his nose then pointed at Cody to let him know he was right.

"Which means I have to use this dangerous welding torch," Cody said, looking at Arwin with a big smile and trying to signal him with his eyes.

But Arwin didn't get the signal.

". . . designed for *adults*," Cody finished.

Now Arwin got it. He nodded knowingly. "Maybe I, an adult, should help you, a child."

"I think that would be acceptable," Cody said.

They high-fived each other.

Arwin couldn't wait to get his hands on Cody's project. He grabbed the welding torch and jumped into Cody's chair. "Whoa! I am going to win this prize!" he said.

"You mean *I'm* going to win that prize," Cody said, confused. Arwin was a little too excited.

"Exactly!" Arwin agreed, firing up the torch. "Because I deserve it."

# Chapter 6

Maddie and London watched Zack pile up his Jesse loot—mostly crumpled towels and socks—on the coffee table in the Martin family suite.

"This should bring in a nice chunk of change," Zack said with satisfaction, holding up the bracelet he had snagged from Jesse's bedside table.

Maddie gasped, totally horrified. "That's Jesse's lucky bracelet," she said.

"How do you know so much about my fiancé?" London asked.

Maddie rolled her eyes. "I'm a journalist. I do my research." Then she turned to Zack. "He never performs without it. Otherwise he could freeze in the middle of his concert, and we'd be responsible for ruining his career."

Now it was London's turn to roll her eyes. Maddie's drama didn't bother her.

"He doesn't need a career," she said, putting air quotes around the word "career." Did she have to point out the obvious? "We'll survive on love . . . and Daddy's money."

"Fine." Zack stepped between them hoping to bring an end to the argument. "I'll just give him the bracelet back and tell him I found it."

The idea of giving up the money he could

get for the bracelet was kind of painful, but he had another, even better idea. "Then I'll ask for his pants as a reward," he said with a grin.

"So your plan is to tell him you found his lucky bracelet in the closed drawer of his bedside table?" Maddie asked.

Was Zack really serious, she wondered? That was the same as admitting he had broken into Jesse's room and stolen the bracelet. No matter how he tried to spin that story, it wouldn't sound good.

But London didn't see a problem. She applauded with a happy smile. "Good plan!"

Maddie sarcastically copied London's applause.

"Bad plan," she said, shaking her head. "If Moseby finds out, we'll all be in trouble. And Zack could end up in jail!"

Zack turned to her with a thoughtful

expression. "Funny, that's what Cody always says."

❖❖❖

The Boston Junior Science Contest was being held in the Tipton Hotel's ballroom. Cody stood next to his laser with a proud smile.

Arwin hovered nearby. He had dressed up for the occasion with a blue-and-white checked jacket over his work overalls. He even tried to find his good pair of glasses, but it turned out that all of Arwin's glasses were held together with tape over the nosepiece.

He checked out the other science projects. Some of them looked pretty good, but they didn't have a chance against his—er, Cody's—laser.

"Wow," Carey said, putting her hand on

Cody's shoulder and checking out his laser. "This is really elaborate. Especially for one day's work."

Arwin responded with a shy laugh. "Thanks," he said. Then he remembered, just in time, that it was actually Cody's project. "You must be really proud of Cody's invention. I mean, finally his talent's being recognized after all these years!"

"He's twelve," Cody's mom said, confused. She was starting to wonder just why Arwin was so proud of Cody's project. But before she could give that too much thought, one of the judges stepped up to the microphone to introduce the science contest finalists. She turned her attention to the stage.

"And now our finalists will demonstrate their projects," he said. "Barbara Brownstein and the science of volcanoes."

Carey gave Cody a look that said, *see, I told you, volcanoes are cool.*

He rolled his eyes.

Barbara stood next to her volcano project. She confidently flipped a switch—but nothing happened. Her self-assured smile wavered a little.

"Um, it's supposed to bubble up and produce ash," she said nervously.

The crowd applauded, but it was lukewarm applause at best. It was pretty clear that Barbara wasn't going to win.

Cody had been nervous up until this point, but he calmed down when he saw the crowd's reaction to the misfiring volcano. "Okay," he said, knocking fists with Arwin. "I feel better now."

Arwin nodded. So did he.

The judge announced the next contestant. "Sheldon Walters."

Sheldon stood next to a human-shaped robot. "My invention is called M.E.C., which stands for My Energy Converter. You put garbage in this end . . ."

Sheldon put a crumpled soda can in the robot's mouth, closed it, and then pushed a button. A lightbulb on top of the robot's head started to glow.

". . . and the robot turns it into energy," Sheldon said proudly. The soda can—now crushed into a small cube—came out of the robot's backside.

The room burst into applause. Real, enthusiastic, prize-winning applause.

Cody was nervous again. "Are you sure this is going to work?" he asked Arwin.

"Of course, I'm sure," Arwin answered with absolute confidence. "I—we—you built it, didn't I—we—you?"

"Our next participant is Mr. Cody

Martin, who will demonstrate his laser," the judge announced.

Cody gave Arwin one last nervous look, then stepped forward. His mother clapped wildly.

Arwin, working as Cody's assistant, set up a piece of metal across the room and then put on a pair of safety goggles.

"I'm going to use this laser to cut a square out of that sheet of metal," Cody told the crowd. "Lights, please?"

Someone dimmed the lights, and Cody flipped the switch on his laser. Cody guided the red beam across the room and cut a square out of the metal. The square of metal hit the floor with a twang.

The room burst into applause again, and Cody stepped back with a smile.

Arwin moved the larger piece of metal aside, and it was only then that the people in the room saw the perfectly square hole in the ballroom's wall! Cody's laser had cut through more than just the metal sheet.

And the audience members weren't the only ones to notice this unexpected hotel renovation! Mr. Moseby glared through the hole, trying to figure out what had happened. His eyes narrowed when he spotted Cody.

Of course, he thought. He should have guessed that one of the Martin twins was behind this!

"Oops! Mr. Moseby!" Cody shouted, trying to duck behind his laser.

But instead, Cody knocked into the laser and accidentally turned it on. The laser's red beam shot around the room, hitting another science fair project called How Mirrors Work.

Sensing danger, everyone in the crowd fell

to the floor. Red laser beams ricocheted wildly around the room, and some of them hit Barbara's volcano. It erupted in a burst of ash and lava before Cody managed to turn off the laser.

Barbara got to her feet. "Ladies and gentlemen, my volcano!" she announced triumphantly.

# Chapter 7

Zack followed Maddie and London out of the air vent and dropped to the floor in Jesse's hotel room. Jesse was under the covers sound asleep.

London stood at the foot of the bed, gazing at him. "He looks so adorable when he's sleeping," she whispered.

"Like an angel," Maddie agreed with a goofy smile on her face.

Jesse rolled over and snorted.

"He even snores beautifully," London said.

Zack tried to bring an end to the lovefest before Jesse woke up.

"Let's focus, people," he whispered urgently. "We'll put the bracelet back, get a couple of shirts, and we're gone." He crossed over to the bedside table, intent on his mission.

Maddie and London stood on either side of the bed, while Zack tried to open the drawer.

"It's stuck," he said, tugging.

Jesse stirred in his sleep, and they all froze.

London leaned over him and started to sing her version of a lullaby. "Hush, little rock star, stay where you are. London's gonna buy you a shiny car."

Jesse smiled, and they all sighed with relief. Maddie kneeled down next to Zack and tried to help. The drawer was really stuck.

"London," she hissed. "Give us a hand, would you?"

But London had other things on her mind.

Maddie looked up to find London on top of the covers next to Jesse. "What are you doing?" she asked.

"I think this is going to be our Christmas/Hanukkah card," London said, whipping out her camera and snapping a picture.

The camera's flash disturbed Jesse's sleep, making him roll over. He threw his arms out and the next thing Maddie knew, she was trapped in his arms.

"Hey, get away from my boyfriend," London demanded.

"I can't move," Maddie whispered.

"Likely story."

"It's not a story," Maddie answered. "It's the truth."

Then she rested her head on Jesse's chest and smiled a contented smile. She couldn't move, but that wasn't necessarily a bad thing.

"But while I'm here, could you take a picture of us?" she asked London.

"No," London snapped, crossing her arms. Why would she take a picture of Maddie with Jesse? After all, *she* was Jesse's girl.

"Zack, take a picture of us," Maddie said.

Zack was still struggling with the drawer. "I'm kind of busy here," he said, irritated. He gave the drawer one more tug, and it flew out and hit the floor with a loud bang.

Everything in it spilled out onto the carpet.

Startled, London jumped back and hit her hand on the window. The window shade rolled up with a loud *thwack*.

The noise and the sunlight that suddenly filled the room woke Jesse up. He sat up in bed and saw the people around him. "What's going on?" he asked, still half asleep.

London smiled at him and stepped toward the bed. "Hi, you don't know me, but we're going to be married," she said.

That woke Jesse up.

"Security!" he yelled.

"Run!" Maddie shouted, heading for the chair under the vent.

Two big security guards opened the door and ran into the room.

London ran, too, snapping pictures as she went. The flash blinded Jesse and the guards, giving the girls enough time to climb up into the vent before they got caught—or worse, Mr. Moseby found out they had broken his rules.

But Zack wasn't as lucky. He was blinded by London's flash, too. He backed up right into the security guards, and the next thing he knew they had each grabbed an arm and were holding him firmly. He couldn't escape. "Hey! Hey! Let me go," Zack yelled.

"Throw him out of here, fellas," Jesse said, pointing to the door.

The guards started to carry Zack out, but he was still holding Jesse's lucky bracelet.

"Wait a minute!" Zack yelled. Considering he was here to do a good thing, he wasn't being treated very well. "I was only in here trying to return your lucky bracelet," he said desperately.

"Return?" Jesse said sarcastically, taking

it from him. "Don't you mean steal?"

"No," Zack protested, shaking his head. "You see, I stole it earlier when you went to the bathroom and Moseby went to get you towels. And by the way, as long as we're confessing, I stole those, too."

Jesse's jaw dropped. "How many times have you been in here?" he asked. What about that great security Mr. Moseby had told him about?

"A couple," Zack admitted. "At least I wasn't pawing through your drawers like my wacky friends."

"You hang with those girls?" Jesse asked, curious.

Zack nodded. He could hear the interest in Jesse's voice, but he didn't understand it. What was the big deal, he wondered. After all, he hung with Maddie and London all the time.

"What are they, like, two years older than you?" Jesse asked.

"Three," Zack answered. He didn't think that the difference in their ages mattered too much, but Jesse clearly did.

"Impressive, dude," Jesse said, knocking Zack's fist. He signaled the guards. "Let him down, guys."

They lowered Zack to the floor and left the room.

"Are girls always after you like this?" Zack asked.

"Yeah. It gets kinda weird," Jesse said.

"Really?"

Jesse sat on his bed with a smile. "No," he said. He really couldn't complain about all those pretty girls chasing after him. "No," he said again. "Fame is pretty cool, but it comes at a price."

Zack nodded understandingly. But what

Jesse had said gave him another idea . . . "Speaking of price, are you finished with that pillowcase?"

Jesse stared at him. Did this kid actually want to sell his pillowcase?

"Sorry, you were saying?" Zack said.

Jesse sighed. He didn't want to complain, but sometimes he just wanted to be a regular guy again. "I was just . . . sometimes I feel like I don't get to do regular stuff," he said wistfully. "You know, shoot hoops, play video games."

Zack brightened. Video games were something he knew about. "If you like video games, come back to my place and I'll crush you like the pretty boy that you are," he challenged.

Jesse wasn't about to turn down a dare. "You're on," he said, grabbing his shoes. "And that's *Mr.* Pretty Boy to you."

# Chapter 8

In the ballroom, the judges were getting ready to announce the first-prize winner of Boston's Junior Science Contest. Sheldon stood onstage with his robot and the second-place ribbon. Cody and Arwin exchanged anxious glances.

"We are so going to win!" Arwin said.

Carey came up behind her son. "Whatever happens, Cody," she said, putting her

arm around him. "I'm very proud of you."
She paused, then added meaningfully, "Mostly
because you did this all by yourself."

Cody stared at the floor. He hadn't done
his project by himself, and he could tell by
the tone of her voice that his mom had figured that out.

Carey turned to Arwin. "Right, Arwin?"
she asked pointedly.

"Yes," Arwin said. He couldn't meet her
eye, either. Cody and Arwin exchanged hope-
ful, nervous looks.

"And our winner is . . . Cody Martin!" the
judge announced.

"Yes!" Arwin yelled, jumping up and
down and pumping his fist in the air. They
had done it!

Cody ran up to the stage to get the
first-place trophy. He held it over his head
in victory. "I'd like to thank the judges for

awarding me this prize," he said.

He looked out over the audience and saw Arwin's wistful expression. He couldn't let this moment pass without giving his friend the props he deserved.

"I'd also like to thank my friend Arwin for . . ." Cody hesitated. What could he say that wouldn't give away their secret? ". . . letting me use his office."

Carey shot her son a look.

Cody saw that look and knew that she wasn't totally buying this heart-warming little speech. He thought fast and added, "I'd also like to thank my mother for being so supportive."

Carey arched her eyebrows. She couldn't support her son for taking credit for Arwin's project.

"And not being judgmental," Cody continued.

But his mom's expression didn't change. If anything, she narrowed her eyes in a way that said, *don't think I'm not on to you!*

Cody's guilt got bigger and bigger. "And loving me even though I lied to her, and I . . ." Now Cody totally broke down. He had cheated and broken the rules. He didn't deserve the award, and now he had to tell the truth. The look on his mother's face left him no choice.

"I don't deserve this prize! I cheated. I had an adult's help."

He stopped talking and looked at Arwin. Was he really an adult? "Well, Arwin's help," he said, correcting himself. "He really deserves this trophy."

Arwin yelped with joy and ran to the stage. He had wanted to win a science contest his entire life.

He grabbed the trophy. "I, I, I . . . wow!"

he sputtered, gazing at the trophy. "Thank you, thank you. It is so nice to be recognized by the scientific community!" He turned to the other winners. "In your face, Sheldon!" he mocked. "Nice volcano, Barbara. Dormant!"

The judges whispered to each other, looking concerned. Finally, the head judge stepped forward. "Excuse me, sir. This competition is for children fourteen and under. How old are you?"

"Thirteen," Arwin said, trying to speak in a high-pitched voice that sounded more kidlike.

The judge simply stared at him. That was obviously a big, fat lie.

"All right," Arwin admitted. "And a half."

The judge shook his head. "You are disqualified," he told Arwin.

"No, please don't," Arwin said, holding on tight to the trophy.

He couldn't believe another science prize was being taken away from him. He hadn't even blown anything up this time! True, there was a little hole in the wall—but it was just a *little* hole. . . .

The judge tried to pull the trophy away from Arwin, but Arwin pulled back. The judge refused to let go. So did Arwin. Finally, Cody moved forward to break up the tug-of-war and escort a weeping Arwin from the stage.

"Our new winner is Sheldon Walters," the judge announced.

"Cody, I am so proud of you for doing the right thing," his mother said. "How do you feel?"

"Better than Arwin," Cody said, patting his friend on the back.

"I'm fine," Arwin insisted. As a scientist, he had to acknowledge others' good work, so he added, through his tears: "It was a beautiful robot."

❖❖❖

Zack and Jesse were kicking back and playing video games. As Zack celebrated his latest win, Jesse said, "Man, you're really good at this."

"Don't feel bad, dude," Zack told him smugly. "We all have to get old sometime."

Maddie and London were knocking on the door. The guys ignored them.

"Jesse?" Maddie yelled. "Just tell me your favorite color, for my article." She paused, but there was no answer. "I'm gonna say blue—is that okay?"

"I don't care what your favorite color is,"

London shouted through the door. "I just want to marry you!"

But wait, she thought, what if his favorite color was totally gross, or worse—one that didn't look good on her. "It's not brown, is it?" she asked.

# Radio Disney

# Your music. Your way.

**Now, there are five fun ways to listen to Radio Disney!**

▶◀**1**)) *On Your Radio...*
Go to RadioDisney.com to find your station

▶◀**2**)) *On Your Computer...*
Stream Radio Disney LIVE on RadioDisney.com or on
iTunes (Radio Area: Top 40/Pop)

▶◀**3**)) *On Your TV...*
Via DirectTV's XM music channel

▶◀**4**)) *On Satellite Radio...*
Go to Channel 115 on XM or Sirius satellite radio

▶◀**5**)) *On Your Mobile Phone...*
Listen to Sprint Radio (Sprint) and MobiRadio (Cingular)

**RadioDisney.com**